I0743078

# Snow Moon

*Nancy M. Bell*

# Snow Moon

**Radical Bookshop and Press**
**4838 Richard Road SW, Suite 300**
**Calgary, AB T3E 6L1**



FIC029000 - Fiction, Short Stories



Chinook Blast Collection
Volume 1
February 1, 2021

Editors: Lexie Angelo
Cover Design: Lexie Angelo

**ISBN-13:** 978-1-990201-07-3

Printed in the United States

Typeset in Pragmatica

*To those who speak and care
for the abandoned and injured
animals who have no voice.*

# contents

# Snow Moon

Sap snapped in the thin branches overhead. Frigid arctic air froze the tiny trickle of life beneath the bark, and black shadows snaked across the moonlit snow at Sydney's feet. Above the frost-bound prairie the brilliant orb of the full moon shed silvery light.

Beneath Sydney's boots, dry snow squeaked as she pushed further into the thicket. Ice formed on her lashes and the sides of her nostrils which stuck together when she inhaled the minus-thirty-degree air. A small shape lay in a blue-shadowed hollow under the bush to her right. Sydney leaned down and scooped up a brown sparrow in her palm. She deposited the bird in the inner pocket of her down jacket and hastily zipped it back up. The poor thing might be dead already, or only overcome by the cold. If it was frozen it wouldn't hurt to carry it, and if it still had a shot at living, the warmth from her body would give it a chance to survive.

She must be crazy to be out here in the middle of the night. The stars wavered starkly in the clear sable sky. There was no cloud cover to hold a tiny bit of warmth near the ground. It was too cold to snow.

Sydney backed out of a tangled web of diamond willow and dogwood and turned to scan the undulating prairie to the west. Her heartbeat echoed in silence as footsteps came nearer. She cursed herself for being a fool. Her trail was sharply etched in the blue silver snow, leading whoever it was straight to where she hid in the low trees.

Eyes narrowed against the cold, she peered through the screen of interlaced twigs. Without warning someone grasped her shoulder from behind. Her hand raised to strike, she whirled to face the heavily muffled figure.

"Sydney, for God's sake what are doing out here?" Sam's voice was incredulous and angry at the same time. "I thought you were a poacher after the deer."

White mist frosted the air between them as she released a huge breath of relief. She shivered and moved further into the bushes to avoid the slight breath of wind that touched her face with a searing icy sword.

"I'm looking for Snow. Millie called and said James threw the white dog out of the shed to make room for his snowmobile." She coughed, her throat protesting the cold air.

"The dog will find somewhere to hole up," said Sam, as he took her elbow and drew her toward the road where her car waited.

Sydney dug her heels in and pulled him to a halt.

"Snow is pregnant, due any day. She'll freeze, and if she doesn't, the puppies will when she whelps. The cold front isn't supposed to move for at least a week." She gripped his arm and stared into his eyes that glittered black in the moonlight. "You know what'll happen..."

"Yup." He grunted. "Where have you looked already?" A resigned smile lifted the corners of his mouth.

"Just this clump of bushes and a bit near Millie's."

10

"I saw your car parked there twenty minutes ago. It's too cold to stay out here much longer." Hard fingers gripped her arm and Sam dragged her toward the road.

"But, Snow..." The words trailed off, her fingers wouldn't work properly, aching with the cold, and she pawed ineffectually at her scarf.

"We'll find the damn dog, I'd just rather not freeze to death before we do," he muttered and continued toward the parked vehicle.

Sydney followed reluctantly, the snow was half-way to her knees and her legs felt wooden and painful from the piercing cold. Sam stopped abruptly and swung her up into his arms. She let out a squeak of surprise although she didn't struggle. Maybe she had stayed out a tad too long.

Sam set her on the ground when they reached the car and held out his hand for her keys. She fumbled at the dome on her jacket pocket. With a muttered oath, the man shoved her fingers away and delved into the pocket himself. The hand withdrew and he turned his back to open the door.

Sydney crawled awkwardly onto the seat. The earlier pain in her hands and lower body was gone. Idly, the thought crossed her mind she should be worried about that fact. Sam's presence filled the car and made it seem small. He inserted the key in the ignition and the engine roared to life.

"Thank God, you have the sense to come out here with a full tank of fuel," he said.

 Feeling somewhat disconnected from the present, she heard him curse again and then put the car in gear. He backed out of the gateway and headed toward his house.

"Snow — we didn't find Snow yet," said Sydney, her words seemed to all run together. "Snow," she tried again. When he didn't pause, she knocked the steering wheel with her hands.

"Stop, for God's sake, woman," Sam growled. "We'll find the dog, but not before you get warm."

"You promise we'll go look for her after I thaw out?" Moonlight threw his features into stark relief when she turned her head to gauge if he was telling the truth.

"Promise. You won't do the dog any good if you're face down in a drift. Nobody would find you 'til spring and by then the coyotes will have had a good feed," he said, his voice gruff.

"You'd find me," Sydney muttered. "You *did* find me."

"Try asking for help before you go haring off across the prairie in weather like this," he said, his voice softening. "You know I always have time to help out. I got an injured dog at the house right now."

"Which one?" Sydney perked up.

"The big shepherd that was hanging out at the casino. Jason shot him 'cause they couldn't catch him, and he wouldn't scat."

"Harvey? They shot Harvey?" Her voice sharpened and sorrow gathered in her chest. "How bad is it?"

"Caught him in the shoulder; hit the bone but I don't think it broke anything."

Sam brought her car to a halt by the back door of his house. He got out and came around to Sydney's door, pulled it open and he carried her toward the house.

Sydney closed her eyes and buried her face in his shoulder. The insides of her eyelids were cold. Could eyes freeze, she wondered aimlessly before her thoughts skittered away. The mudroom was blessedly warm when Sam shouldered their way through the entry. Without stopping he continued on into the kitchen, pushing the adjoining door open and then closed with his foot.

Her face burned in the heated air and she raised a hand to rub her cheeks as he set her on a wing chair near the wood stove. Sam caught her hand.

"Don't touch your face 'til it warms up some. You got a bit of frostbite, but it should be okay if you don't rub it." He waited until she nodded before releasing her hand.

"Where's Harvey?"

Sydney removed her mitts and scarf, but her face still burned and itched. She needed something to distract her from the discomfort of her warming body. A tail thumped on the floor behind her.

"Behind you. He's coming along pretty good."

Sam made a cup of tea and handed it to Sydney as she wrapped her chilled hands around the warm pottery, closing her eyes against the sharp tingling in her fingers. A chair scraped, and the table moved slightly, as Sam sat across from her. She reached inside her jacket and pulled out a little bird. It stirred in her hand.

"Where'd you get that?" he asked.

"Found it under a bush, maybe it'll be okay. At least it has a chance now."

He took the tiny creature from her palm, placed it in a small cage and set it near the stove.

Harvey thumped his tail on the floor again and Sam offered the dog a biscuit. The big shepherd eyed it for a moment, sniffed it suspiciously and then taking it carefully in his mouth, spat it out onto the cushioned bed he lay on. Satisfied nothing was amiss, he wolfed it down in one gulp.

"Aye, you should chew, man," he said with amusement.

Sydney slipped from her seat and knelt beside the large tri-coloured animal. The top of his huge wedge-shaped head was bigger than her hand. She ran her fingers behind his ear and scratched before sliding down to inspect the shoulder. There was some swelling around the bandage, but no blood marred the covering. Bending close she sniffed and was relieved at the absence of the sickly-sweet smell of pus and infection.

Sam knelt beside her, gentle hands loosened the dressing and pulled it away. The bullet hole was clean, a round gaping hole in the patch of shaved hide. The edges of the wound were bright red, seeping a little blood and clear serum.

"Is the bullet out?" Sydney accepted the cloth soaked in antiseptic and wiped the site before handing it back and taking the tube of antibiotic cream. She coated the area with the ointment and handed the tube back to him. She wiped her hands on a towel and sat back to let Sam put a new dressing on.

"Yeah, it came out easy enough. Bruised the bone some though."

"Did you talk to the vet over at Eagle Mountain?

"I called Dr. Carl. He gave me some penicillin and checked the wound after I got the bullet out," Sam reassured her.

"It wouldn't kill them to do some pro bono work, but I guess they gotta make a living too."

A gust of wind hit the window, windblown snow hissed and whispered around the eaves. She stood up and reached for her mitts.

"I'm warm enough now, let's go find Snow. If she whelps with this wind the poor things will freeze before they get all the way born." Sydney wound her scarf around her head. Her thoughts involuntarily straying to the litter she found earlier in the week. The momma's teats were frostbitten, three puppies barely alive and three more frozen to the side of the makeshift shelter. Not Snow's puppies, she vowed.

"Hang on, I'll call Millie and see if she's seen her," he offered. "It's a good thing she keeps an eye on all the strays and lets us know when one of them is hurt or needs help."

"Let's hope," she agreed without much enthusiasm.

Sam's voice rumbled in the other room while he spoke on the phone. He entered the kitchen, set a bowl of food in front of Harvey and gave him quick pat on the head.

"Be good and don't wreck the place while I'm gone," he joked.

"What did Millie say?" Sydney asked.

"She didn't think the dog would go far. James has been trying to run her off for weeks now and she keeps coming back."

"Maybe she's holed up around the buildings somewhere. I did look there at first, but James scares the crap out of me at night. When's he's drinking he'll shoot at anything," Sydney spoke over her shoulder as they left the building.

"He ain't a bad guy, Sydney. He just gets a little trigger happy when he's drunk," Sam said, defending the old man.

"Yeah well, it's just I prefer my hide without holes in it," she replied tartly.

Sam slid into the driver seat. The exhaust rose in a vertical plume toward the star specked sky.

Sam put the truck in gear and drove out the lane. Millie and James' place was a quarter mile down the gravel road. Wild yipping and drawn-out high-pitched howls echoed in the air. The wind blew fitfully, throwing snow devils across the fields.

"Sounds like the 'yotes have got a kill," Sam observed.

"Let's hope it isn't Snow," Sydney said grimly. "I've been trying to bring her into the shelter since the fall, but she's too smart to get caught."

He turned the truck into the narrow, rutted lane with diamond willow crowding the sides. Lights were on in the house at the top of the high-centred drive. There was no use in asking for help. Millie wouldn't have let her husband know she talked to Sam about the dog. Sam parked in the shadow of the old barn. The structure tilted drunkenly to the southeast.

Sydney left the truck, careful not to slam the door. No need to have anyone out here wondering why they were scrounging around in the sheds. She hoped the whine of the wind would hide the sound of the motor. Rusty hinges squealed shrilly when Sam pulled the door open. Old machinery and junk littered the interior. Moonlight fell in irregular stripes across the mess.

"Snow, there's a good girl, are you here?" Sam called into the barn, his breath ghosting around his head in the frigid air.

"Snow, where's my girl?" Sydney entreated.

They stood in silence, listening for the slightest sound but only the scurry of tiny mice greeted them.

"She's not here. She always comes to me," Sydney said as they left the building, shoving the door shut behind them.

Two granaries stood behind the barn, and old truck caps were strewn about under the winter-bare aspen trees. Sam moved to check beneath the caps where the feral dogs often took refuge. Sydney checked both granaries, the doors flapping slightly in the wind. The first one held nothing more than the leg bone of a moose, gnawed on and discarded by whichever dog had dragged it there. The second was empty as well. She glanced toward Sam who straightened up from the cap he was peering into and shook his head.

"Dammit," she cursed. Her fingers were freezing again, the tips already dead to the touch. She closed her eyes for a moment and held her breath. Who would have ever guessed that breathing could sound so loud in the silence? She detected nothing beyond the rustle of the few dead leaves still clinging to the bare branches and the sibilant sound of snow slipping across the frozen surface on the wind's breath.

Sam moved toward her and pointed at an old structure closer to the house. He held his finger to his lips. Sydney followed in his wake only to find it was an empty abandoned outhouse.

Near the outhouse was an old shed but before they reached it, a door banged—the noise echoing sharply in the stillness. Sam grabbed her arm and pulled her into the shadow of the building. The hens in the coop near the house raised an alarm, screeching and flapping their wings loudly. A man's voice cut through the cacophony, followed by the report of a gun. The hens fell silent and four dark shapes raced across the moonlit snow.

"Damn coyotes," the man cursed.

The throaty roar of the shotgun vibrated in the night.

Footsteps crunched across the broken snow by the house and a door slammed shut. Sydney's feet were rapidly growing dangerously cold again, but she followed Sam toward the shed. He pulled the broken door open slightly and slid through. Sydney was reluctant to take the chance of being caught in the building, so she checked the leeward side of the structure, searching behind the boards and piles of junk.

Desperation drove her out into the light on the side closest the house. As she worked her way to the back end a small noise caught her attention. She dropped to her knees and dug under an old sofa covered with a tarp.

"Snow," she whispered. "Good girl, are you here, dog?"

An almost inaudible whine came from deeper under the tarp. Sydney wriggled further into the opening. It was a good thing it was winter; the stench of the animal was horrible even in the cold. It took two baths and ten days of decent food to get the stink off the dogs she rescued.

She stretched her hand out toward the sound, hoping it wasn't a coyote, or a dog she didn't know, hidden there. Her reaching fingers encountered something solid. Investigating with her hand she identified a leg and a paw.

"Snow, c'mon girl. Come toward me," she pleaded.

She took hold of the two paws she could reach and pulled gently. The dog grunted but made no move to bite her. The cold body slid toward her and she realized she had the hind legs. When she inspected her mitt in the dim light, it was covered with a dark fluid, but it was hard to tell what. She pulled again and the dog scrabbled with her front paws, pushing backward toward Sydney.

"Sydney, where are you?" Sam whispered harshly.

"Here, under the tarp on this gross sofa," she whispered back.

"Did you find her, then?"

"I found somebody, I've got her back end and it's too dark to tell who it is," Sydney replied.

"Can you manage?"

"I think so. I've almost got her free. She crawled down into the springs."

She wriggled further from under the crackling tarp and heaved the dog toward her. Whatever had been impeding the progress let go abruptly and Sydney fell on her back, the dog clutched in her arms.

"It's her," Sam said.

The dog opened her eyes wearily and then closed them again.

Sam leaned down and lifted the heavy weight from her chest. He cradled the animal, opened his jacket and wrapped it around the cold creature. Sydney scrambled to her feet and ran ahead of him to open the back door of the truck. Welcome heat fanned across her skin as she flung it wide. Sam was only seconds behind her and deposited his burden on the backseat.

"She hasn't whelped yet, so we don't have to go crawl back in there looking for puppies," he said.

"Thank God for that, it was not high on my list of things I want to do right now."

She climbed into the passenger side and was barely seated before Sam had the truck in gear and rolling down the lane. Minutes later, he turned into his drive and stopped by the back door. Snow lifted her head from the seat and curled her lip, but soon she dropped her head back onto her paws.

Sam opened the door and scooped the dog up in one movement. Sydney jumped down and ran ahead to open the door to the house. Once in the house, she followed Sam into the kitchen. Harvey scrabbled to his feet, a growl building in his chest. Sam placed Snow on a heap of pillows near the warm stove.

"Hush now, you," he admonished the big shepherd. "It's Snow, you fool. These are probably your puppies in her belly."

Sydney ran her hand over Snow's distended abdomen. A contraction rippled under her hand. Sam carefully tended to the frostbite on the pads of her feet. Harvey nudged his head between the humans to confirm Snow was indeed a pack mate before he hobbled back to his bed where he lay down with a grunt.

"I think the puppies are ready to come." Sydney spoke in a low voice.

"Cover her with this," he said pulling a blanket out of the just-warm oven. "She's just about frozen stiff, poor beast."

Sydney covered the dog as shivers shook the emaciated body. She tucked the thick blanket over the frozen ears leaving only Snow's muzzle sticking out.

Snow grunted and her body convulsed. The sharp smell of blood and amniotic fluid filled the room. Sam flipped the material off the dog's hind end. The first puppy slithered out and Sydney slid a thick pad of warmed towels under it. Four more followed in quick order, and Snow lay still, her sides heaving. Sydney exchanged a worried look with Sam who set the puppies close enough so Snow could lick them clean before nudging them toward her teats.

Gusts of wind shook the small house. Sydney placed the sixth puppy with its mates close against Snow's side, warm and snug under the blanket.

"This is one litter that won't freeze to death," she said grimly.

"You can only save one at time, Syd. Don't eat your heart out over things you can't change. Be happy we found this dog in time."

Sam held her gaze and squeezed her hand.

"I know you're right, it's just hard." Sydney swallowed hard and managed a small smile.

The white dog continued to pant and pawed at her frozen ears. Sam and Sydney towel-dried the pups and placed them back with their mother. The squirming mass of tiny bodies burrowed into the soft underbelly searching instinctively for the milk engorged teats.

"It's a miracle she has any milk at all considering how skinny she is," Sydney murmured.

"You know how it is; they give what they have to the babies and survive themselves on the little that's left." Sam smoothed Harvey's head. The big shepherd sat on his haunches beside him overseeing the birth.

She rose to her feet and opened a can of dog food she found on the counter. Emptying it into a bowl, Sydney mixed in some warm water and bits of liver from a container nearby. Harvey

20

lumbered upright, his tail waving like a plume, a doggy smile on his face.

"Not for you, bud." She moved past him and set the dish by Snow's head. The dog's tail thumped the floor under the blanket as she bolted the food without pausing to chew. Harvey sat down with a sigh and whined deep in his throat.

A fresh salvo of blowing snow rattled the windowpane and the large spruce trees around the house soughed louder.

"Sounds like the wind is picking up, I should go while the roads are still passable. They're gonna drift in pretty quick if this keeps up." She swiped the hair out of her face and got to her feet. Her gaze fell on the tiny fluff of feathers huddled in the bottom of the cage by the stove. "What should we do with the bird, do you want me to take it with me?"

"No, leave it here. Once the weather warms up, I'll let it go." Sam stood up too, he raised his arms over his head and stretched. "Man, I am getting too old for sitting on the hard floor in the middle of the night."

"You're younger than me," she scolded him.

"Only by two days," he smirked. "Want some coffee before you head out?" He moved to the coffee maker and poured himself a cup. He waved an empty mug in her direction.

"Can you make it to go? I want to get moving while I still can." She cast a worried look out the frosty window.

"Why don't you drink this, and I'll go check the road at the top of the drive." Sam set the coffee on the table and pressed her into a chair. He drew on his heavy parka and stamped into his snow boots.

A cold draft swirled around her ankles when he left the kitchen. Sydney wrapped her still cold hands around the warm mug and relished the hot coffee as it warmed her from the inside. Harvey laid his head on her lap and she fed him a dog cookie from the jar on the table. Moments later the door rattled, and Sam swept in along with a rush of frigid wind. He removed his gloves and clapped them against each other to knock off the crusted snow.

"The road is drifted two feet deep from the end of the drive all the way to the corner." He removed his coat and hung it by the door.

Sydney got to her feet and looked out the window. The long drive appeared fairly clear, with only a skiff of snow covering it as it wound between the swaying spruce trees. "Doesn't look that bad from here. I think I can make it." She set her cup on the table and started to wind a scarf around her head. The clink of metal hitting the table brought her gaze to Sam's face.

"Once you get out past the shelterbelt the drifts are up to your knees and getting worse."

She picked up the keys and shifted them from one hand to the other with indecision. She really needed to leave, but the thought of fighting the drifts and getting stuck on the road in the freezing night was daunting. As she hesitated, the lights flickered twice and then went out. Somewhere in the dark Sam chuckled. Wavering lamp light followed the scrape of a match and he set the oil lamp on the table.

"You should stay," he said. "I'm gonna bring more wood in from the shed." The door slammed on the last of his words.

Sydney dragged the sofa closer to the stove. She pulled some wool blankets and a couple of quilts from the blanket box next to the wall. Sinking down beside Snow and the puppies she caressed the dog's head and examined her ears. The dog whined softly as she touched the tender flesh. It looked like some of the edges might slough off, but most of the ears would be saved. Lifting the blanket, Sydney checked on the sleeping puppies. All seemed fine, the little bellies rounded and full.

Sam came in and deposited a load of wood in the box by the fire. "That should do us for the night," he said before stripping off his outer clothes. Opening the stove, he added another log and then moved to the fireplace on the other side of the room. Soon, he had a fire blazing in the hearth and the temperature in the room rose noticeably. He settled on the sofa and pulled a wool blanket around himself. He reached down and took Sydney's hand pulling her up on the cushion beside him.

"Just like when we camped out when we were kids," he said softly.

"It's been a long time since we were kids, Sam."

Smiling, he enfolded her in his blanket, pulling her body against his solid warmth. With his other hand he spread more blankets over them.

"This is nicer than being snowed in alone," Sam murmured.

Sydney agreed.

## ABOUT THE AUTHOR

Nancy lives near Balzac, Alberta with her husband and various critters. She is a member of the Writers Guild of Alberta. Nancy has presented at the Surrey International Writers Conference, at the Writers Guild of Alberta Conference, When Words Collide and Word on the Lake. She has publishing credits in poetry, fiction and non-fiction. Nancy is also active in animal rescue and volunteers with Alberta Animal Rescue Crew Society in Calgary, AB.

## SPECIAL THANKS

Chinook Blast Festival

The City of Calgary

Tourism Calgary

Calgary Municipal Land Corporation

Calgary Arts Development

Calgary Public Library

IngramSpark